WE'RE ON OUR WAY TO SEE KING BEAR

**Written and illustrated by fifth-grade students
of Holly Springs Elementary School in Pickens, South Carolina**

Mrs. Patsy Smith, Teacher/Project Coordinator

SCHOLASTIC INC.
New York Toronto London Auckland Sydney
Mexico City New Delhi Hong Kong

Once upon a time, in a deep, dark forest in the Jocassee Gorges, there lived a raccoon named Rusty. Rusty was tumbling and rolling in the nasty mud with his best friend, Butch Bobcat.

Rusty said, "I'm getting hungry! Do you want to eat supper at my house?"

"Yeah!" said Butch. "Let's go wash up!"

They went to the riverbank and dove into the cool water. As they splashed to the surface, the mud started to rinse off their faces and drip into the river.

"There's still mud around your eyes, Rusty!" Butch said. Rusty dipped his head beneath the water and scrubbed around his eyes.

"Is that better?" he asked.

"Sorry, Rusty, you still look like you're wearing a mask! But I don't think it will wash off."

Rusty found a still pool of water and looked at his reflection. Sure enough, there was a black mask on his face.

"I think that has always been there," Rusty said. "I know how we can find out!"

Rusty and Butch ran to Rusty's house, and Rusty pulled out his photo album. "Yep," Butch said, "you've always worn a mask. I wonder why!"

"I've never really thought about it before," said Rusty, "but I would like to know. I don't like things that make me different!"

"I know what you mean, Rusty! I have these spots all over me! I look like I have a disease or something!" Butch said.

OCONEE STATE PARK **FOOTHILLS TRAIL** Horse Pasture River

Burrell's Ford Whitewater Falls

Toxaway River
Suspension Bridge

Laurel Fork
Falls

Sassafras
Mountain

TABLE
ROCK

Rusty and Butch were very quiet during supper. They didn't eat much. They just pushed their food around on their plates.

All of a sudden, Rusty exclaimed, "Hey! Why don't we go see King Black Bear and ask him why we have these problems? He's the wisest animal in the Kingdom."

"That's a great idea, Rusty!" Butch agreed. "Let's go first thing in the morning."

Rusty and Butch woke up bright and early the next morning and packed their gear for a long hike. They set out to find the Foothills Trail, which goes from one end of the Jocassee Gorges to the other. Their destination was Table Rock, where King Black Bear ruled the animal kingdom. They found the sign,

and started their journey. As they walked, they sang this song (to the tune of "Camptown Races"):

> *We're on our way to see King Bear,*
> *Doo-dah, doo-dah,*
> *He'll answer all our questions there,*
> *Oh, doo-dah day.*
> *Gonna walk all night—gonna walk all day,*
> *Hiking on the Foothills Trail, singing all the way.*

Toxaway River
Suspension Bridge

Laurel Fork
Falls

Sassafras
Mountain

TABLE
ROCK

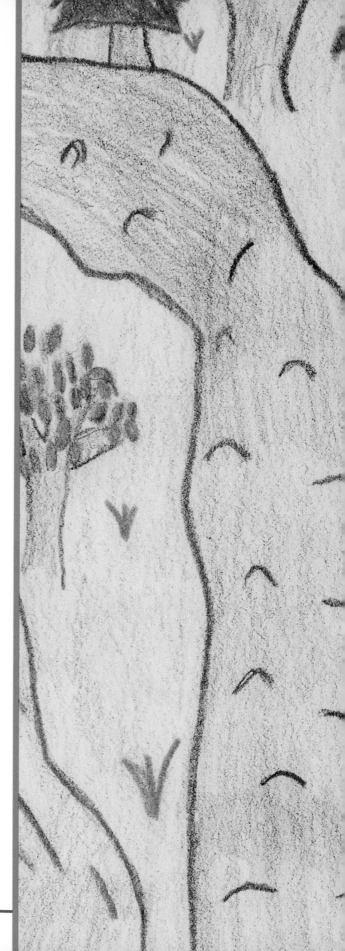

They stopped to get a drink at Burrell's Ford on the Chattooga River, when they heard a noise coming from the briar patch.

"Ouch! Ow!"

They went over to investigate. They saw a rabbit trying to untangle her ears from a long briar.

"Do you need some help?" they asked.

"No thanks, I do this all the time. You would too if you had ears like these!" she said. "My name is Rebecca Rabbit. What's yours?"

"My name's Rusty Raccoon and this is my best friend, Butch Bobcat. We're on our way to see King Bear to ask him some important questions."

"Like what?" Rebecca asked, as she finally freed her ears.

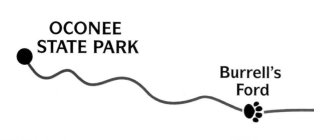

OCONEE STATE PARK

Burrell's Ford

"Like why I wear a mask," said Rusty.

"And why I'm covered with spots," said Butch. "We don't like being different from the other animals!"

"Neither do I!" Rebecca agreed. "May I come with you to ask why I have such long ears?"

"Sure! Come along!" Rusty and Butch said.

So Rebecca packed her gear and joined them. They found the sign,

and started their journey. As they walked, they sang this song:

We're on our way to see King Bear,
Doo-dah, doo-dah,
He'll answer all our questions there,
Oh, doo-dah day.
Gonna walk all night—gonna walk all day,
Hiking on the Foothills Trail, singing all the way.

When they got to Whitewater Falls, they noticed that their canteens were almost empty. "We can refill them here, but be very careful!" Rusty warned.

Rebecca stepped out onto a rock to get closer to the water, when she slipped and fell into the rushing stream. "Help! Somebody help me, please!" she shouted.

Butch was downstream and heard her cries. Thinking quickly, he climbed out on a limb hanging over the falls, reached down, and grabbed Rebecca by the ears. "I've got you, Rebecca," he said.

"Thanks, Butch," Rebecca said, as she was once again on dry land.

They carefully filled the rest of their canteens and once again were on their way.

OCONEE STATE PARK

FOOTHILLS TRAIL

Burrell's Ford

Whitewater Falls

Horse Pasture River

Toxaway River
Suspension Bridge

Laurel Fork
Falls

Sassafras
Mountain

TABLE
ROCK

They had been walking for quite a while. "My feet are killing me!" Butch said.

"Mine, too!" the others echoed.

So they stopped at Horse Pasture River to loosen their boot strings.

"Wow! Look at that red bush," Rusty said.

"Is it already Christmas?" Rebecca asked.

"No, but I think I see berries on it. Let's go pick some!" Rusty said.

Rusty walked over and reached for the bush. To his surprise, the bush yelped!

"If you want to pick berries, fine—but hairballs on my bushy tail— I don't think so!" someone said.

"You have a berry bush on your tail?" Rusty asked.

"No, that berry bush IS MY TAIL!" The bush turned and Rusty saw that it was a fox.

"I am so sorry," Rusty said. "I didn't mean to hurt your feelings."

"That's okay," the fox said. "When you have a tail like this, you get used to it. I didn't mean to snap at you. My name is Frankie Fox."

"My name is Rusty Raccoon, and these are my friends, Butch Bobcat and Rebecca Rabbit. We're on our way to see King Bear to ask him some important questions."

OCONEE
STATE PARK

FOOTHILLS TRAIL

Horse Pasture
River

Burrell's
Ford

Whitewater
Falls

"Like what?" Frankie asked, as he picked a hairball from his tail.

"Like why I wear a mask," said Rusty.

"And why I'm covered with spots," said Butch.

"And why I have long ears," said Rebecca. "We don't like being different from the other animals!"

"Neither do I," Frankie said. "May I come with you to ask why I have such a bushy tail?"

"Sure! Come along!" Rusty, Butch, and Rebecca said.

Frankie packed his hiking equipment and joined them. They found the sign,

and started on their journey. As the walked, they sang this song:

We're on our way to see King Bear,
Doo-dah, doo-dah,
He'll answer all our questions there,
Oh, doo-dah day.
Gonna walk all night—gonna walk all day,
Hiking on the Foothills Trail, singing all the way.

Toxaway River
Suspension Bridge

Laurel Fork
Falls

Sassafras
Mountain

TABLE
ROCK

"I'm really tired, Rusty," Frankie said, "Let's stop for the night!"

"Okay, if everyone agrees," said Rusty. "Who wants to spend the night at the Toxaway River Suspension Bridge?"

Everyone said, "Yes, I do!" except Rebecca, who was afraid of high places.

"Oh, come on, Rebecca," Butch coaxed. "We'll all be together. There's nothing to be afraid of!"

"Okay," Rebecca agreed.

They all got out their sleeping bags and settled down for a good night's sleep.

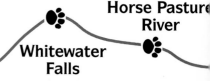

OCONEE STATE PARK

FOOTHILLS TRAIL

Burrell's Ford

Whitewater Falls

Horse Pasture River

Toxaway River
Suspension Bridge

Laurel Fork
Falls

Sassafras
Mountain

TABLE
ROCK

OCONEE STATE PARK

FOOTHILLS TRAIL

Burrell's Ford

Whitewater Falls

Horse Pasture River

The next morning the group of friends continued their journey. After a while, Frankie said, "I'm hungry. Let's stop for lunch!" So they stopped beside Laurel Fork Falls for a picnic.

Rusty said, "I smell something. Whose food stinks?"

Butch said, "It's Rebecca's carrots! Yuck!"

"No, it is NOT my carrots," Rebecca answered.

"It's not Rebecca's carrots. It's me," a voice said.

"Where did that voice come from?" Frankie whispered.

"From the waterfall, I think," Rusty said, and started walking in that direction. Suddenly, a little black and white skunk stepped from behind the falls.

"Hi," she said shyly, "I'm Sunny Skunk, and I have a stinking problem."

"Don't worry, Sunny. We all have problems. My name is Rusty Raccoon, and these are my friends, Butch Bobcat, Rebecca Rabbit, and Frankie Fox. We're on our way to see King Bear to ask him some important questions."

"Like what?" Sunny asked, wiping water droplets from her forehead.

Toxaway River Suspension Bridge

Laurel Fork Falls

Sassafras Mountain

TABLE ROCK

OCONEE
STATE PARK

FOOTHILLS TRAIL

Burrell's
Ford

Whitewater
Falls

Horse Pasture
River

"Like why I wear a mask," said Rusty.

"And why I'm covered with spots," said Butch.

"And why I have long ears," said Rebecca.

"And why I have such a bushy tail," said Frankie. "We don't like being different from the other animals!"

"Neither do I," Sunny said. "May I come with you to ask why I have a stinking problem?"

"Sure! Come along!" Rusty, Butch, Rebecca, and Frankie said.

Sunny gathered her hiking gear (and deodorant), and joined them. They found the sign,

and started their journey. As they walked, they sang this song:

> *We're on our way to see King Bear,*
> *Doo-dah, doo-dah,*
> *He'll answer all our questions there,*
> *Oh, doo-dah day.*
> *Gonna walk all night—gonna walk all day,*
> *Hiking on the Foothills Trail, singing all the way.*

Toxaway River Suspension Bridge

Laurel Fork Falls

Sassafras Mountain

TABLE ROCK

Following the Foothills Trail up Sassafras Mountain, the group was getting closer to their final destination, Table Rock. All was going well, when they saw a strange group ahead of them.

"Oh, look at the little babies!" one of the strangers said. "Is nursery school on a field trip?"

The others laughed as he walked over to Frankie. He started to grab Frankie's backpack, when Sunny said, "Leave him alone!"

"Says who?"

"Says ME!" And with that, Sunny turned around, lifted her tail into the air, and sent a spray directly at him.

The strangers took off through the woods.

"Thank you, Sunny. You saved my life!" Frankie said.

"You would have done the same thing for me, Frankie. It was nothing," Sunny said.

OCONEE STATE PARK

FOOTHILLS TRAIL

Burrell's Ford

Whitewater Falls

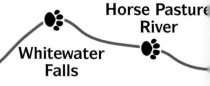

Horse Pasture River

Toxaway River
Suspension Bridge

Laurel Fork
Falls

Sassafras
Mountain

TABLE
ROCK

They had been walking for a long time when they came upon the sign,

They all let out a sigh of relief. "I am so glad we made it!" Butch exclaimed. "I thought we would never get here!"

"It took a lot of teamwork," Rusty said. "We would never have made it if we hadn't worked together."

As they approached the palace cave of King Black Bear, they saw two guards. Rusty said to one of them, "We would like to see King Bear, please."

"Wait here," the guard ordered and disappeared down the long hallway. When he returned, he said, "His Majesty will see you now. Enter and follow the light."

FOOTHILLS TRAIL

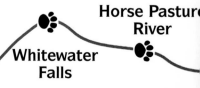

Toxaway River
Suspension Bridge

Laurel Fork
Falls

Sassafras
Mountain

TABLE
ROCK

Rusty and his friends huddled together as they entered the hallway. "Wow," Rebecca said, "this place is so beautiful!"

They walked slowly, and the light guided them. When they entered the huge throne room, King Bear looked up from one of the books on his desk. "What do you want?" he asked.

The others nudged Rusty to the front. "Sir, we have traveled a long, long way to ask you some important questions."

"All right, ask them," the King said.

"I want to know why I wear a mask," Rusty said.

"And why I'm covered with spots," said Butch.

"And why I have long ears," said Rebecca.

"And why I have such a bushy tail," said Frankie.

"And why I have a stinking problem," Sunny said.

"WE DON'T LIKE BEING DIFFERENT FROM THE OTHER ANIMALS!" they all said together.

The King answered, "All the things you named, that you see as problems, are things that serve a very distinct purpose. They help you to survive. They are a part of you, as you are a part of this great Kingdom.

"What if all the flowers decided they wanted to be red? We wouldn't have any yellow honeysuckle blooms or pink mountain laurels. The forest would lose a great deal of its color, wouldn't it?

"It's the same with you. Your unique qualities teach us all to respect individual differences. True wisdom begins when you accept yourselves for who you are, and realize that you are special. No other animal could take your place in this Kingdom. Now, go back to your homes, and be proud of who you are!"

The group was quiet as they left the palace. Once they were back in the forest, Rusty said, "He's right, you know. We have all learned to overlook each other's differences on our trip here and have become good friends. If we like each other, surely we can like ourselves!"

The others all agreed. They started their journey back to their homes. As they walked, they sang this song.

We learned a lot from King Black Bear,
Doo-dah, doo-dah,
We learned to love and trust and care,
Oh, doo-dah day.
Gonna like ourselves — each and every hue —
Together we can build a world that knows we're special, too!

EPILOGUE

Even though this story is fiction, the setting is real. The Jocassee Gorges, comprised of 32,000 acres of forestland, is located in the northwestern corner of South Carolina, practically in our school's backyard. Recently purchased by the state government, discussion is now underway as to how to best use this area. Over 1,200 species of endangered animals have been documented as living in this area. As Rusty and his friends discovered, each animal is unique and deserves a place to live and grow. That's why we feel this area should be protected. We also urge you to help protect the wildlife habitats in your area, too.

Note: In each illustration in our book, look for the Small-footed Myotis (bat), which is one of the Jocassee Gorges' endangered species.

Kids Are Authors®
Books written by children for children

The Kids Are Authors® Competition was established in 1986 to encourage children to read and to become involved in the creative process of writing. Since then, thousands of children have written and illustrated books as participants in the Kids Are Authors® Competition. The winning books in the annual competition are published by Scholastic Inc. and are distributed by Scholastic Book Fairs throughout the United States.

For more information:

Kids Are Authors®
Scholastic Book Fairs
PO Box 958411
Lake Mary, FL 32795-8411

Or visit our web site at
www.scholasticbookfairs.com